SPACE HOPPERS

NURSERY ON NEPTUNE

TOMMY DONBAVAND

NASEN House, 4/5 Amber Business Village, Amber Close, Amington, Tamworth, Staffordshire, B77 4RP

Rising Stars UK Ltd.
7 Hatchers Mews, Bermondsey Street, London SE1 3GS
www.risingstars-uk.com

Published 2014

Author: Tommy Donbavand
Cover design: Sarah Garbett @ Sg Creative Services
Illustrations: Alan Brown for Advocate Art
Text design and typesetting: Sarah Garbett @ Sg Creative Services
Publisher: Fiona Lazenby
Editorial consultants: Jane Friswell and Dee Reid
Editorial: Fiona Tomlinson and Sarah Chappelow

British Library Cataloguing in Publication Data.
A CIP record of this book is available from the British Library.

ISBN: 978-1-78339-325-1

Printed in the UK by Ashford Colour Press Ltd, Gosport, Hampshire

CONTENTS

MEET THE SPACE HOPPERS

DAN

Name: Dan Fireball
Rank: Captain
Age: 12
Home planet: Earth
Most likely to: hide behind the Captain's chair and ask timidly, "Are we there yet?"

ASTRA

Name: Astra Moon
Rank: Second Officer
Age: 11
Home planet: The Moon
Most likely to: face up to The Geezer, strike a karate pose and say, "Bring it on!"

HS INFINITY

THE GEEZER

VOLT

Name: Volt
Rank: Agent
Age: Really old!
Home planet: Venus
Most likely to: puff steam from his shoulder exhausts and announce, "Hop completed!"

GUS

Name: Gus Buster
Rank: Head of COSMIC
Age: 15
Home planet: Earth
Most likely to: suddenly appear on the view screen and yell, "Fireball, where are you?"

VOLT

Greetings new recruits!

My name is Volt and I shall be your cyber-teacher for today.

You should read this section because if you wish to become **COSMIC** agents you must know the history of the Solar System.

Long ago, adults used to be in charge of everything. They had jobs, ran governments and were in charge of television remote controls.

Children were forced to stay in school until the age of 18. They had to do everything their parents told them. They were only given small amounts of currency, known as "pocket money".

There were lots of problems. Adults polluted the Earth and then went on to do the same – or even worse – on the remaining eight planets of our Solar System. In fact, for a long time, adults even refused to call Pluto a real planet!

So, in the year 2281, the children took over.

Adults were made to retire at the age of 18 and were sent to retirement homes on satellites in space. Children just needed three years at school, so most children were working by the time they were eight years old.

The Solar System quickly became a much happier, safer and cleaner place to live.

However, not all of the adults liked having to retire at the age of 18. Some of them rebelled and escaped from their retirement homes on satellites in

space. They began to cause trouble and commit crimes.

That's why **COSMIC** was created:

Crimes

   Of

      Serious

         Magnitude

            Investigation

               Company

The worst of these villains was known as The Geezer. The purpose of COSMIC was to stop The Geezer from committing crimes.

Members of COSMIC flew around the Solar System solving mysteries and bringing badly behaved adults to justice. The COSMIC spaceships could navigate an invisible series of magnetic tunnels called the Hop Field, so they were called Space Hoppers.

I myself, was a member of one such team of Space Hoppers, alongside the famous agents - Dan Fireball and Astra Moon.

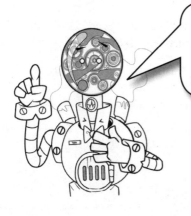

If you turn the page, you can read about the time we got dragged into an adventure on our day off ...

CHAPTER 1

PARTY ON!

HS INFINITY DATA LOG

MISSION REPORT 4:

NURSERY ON NEPTUNE

REPORT BEGINS ...

Second Officer Astra Moon sat behind her desk on the command deck of the HS Infinity and held her palm over a large, yellow button.

She spoke to Volt, the old-fashioned brass robot, "Are the co-ordinates all programmed in?" she asked.

Across the room, Volt blew steam from his twin exhaust pipes and rolled over to a computer terminal on his single wheel. "They are indeed, Miss Astra."

Astra grinned. "Then prepare to Hop!"

She slammed her hand down on the button, and the HS Infinity leapt sideways into one of the invisible magnetic tunnels that make up the Hop Field, connecting every planet and moon in the Solar System. Within seconds, the ship was whizzing along.

"Are you okay, Dan?" Astra cried.

"Couldn't be better!" replied Dan Fireball from his captain's chair at the front of the deck. He stared at a three-dimensional image projecting up from a shimmering cube in his lap.

For a few seconds everything went fuzzy — as though the entire universe was made out of candy floss. Astra clung on to the edge of her desk. Her mouth was dry, and it felt like someone was tickling her all over.

"Hop completed," announced Volt. "We have arrived at Neptune."

Astra smiled. "The perfect place to spend a day off!" she sighed. "No chasing evil adults for us today — just relaxing, catching up with old friends ..."

"... and partying!" exclaimed Dan, jumping up from his seat. He hurried over to Astra and placed the glowing cube in front of her. "This holographic website is awesome!"

Astra looked closer. In the moving image above the cube, she could see a group of small children laughing as they drank from bottles of milk and munched on rusks.

"Welcome to Neptune Nursery!" said a child's voice. "The university where your education flies past by day — and the nights are there to enjoy!"

"Hang on," said Astra, switching off the cube. "We're here to visit my cousin, Honey, and watch her graduate from college — not to hang out with a bunch of nappy-wearing party animals."

"That's the brilliant part!" said Dan. "We can do both! We sit at the boring ceremony and watch Honey collect her certificate or whatever, then get an invitation to the party they hold afterwards. I hear the organisers have the warm milk hopped in especially from Pluto!"

"Now, wait a minute!" said Astra firmly. "You weren't even going to come with me today. Not until I told you that my cousin went to Neptune Nursery!"

"Well, what do you expect me to do?" demanded Dan. "Miss out on my one chance to sample life on the Solar System's greatest party planet? Nursery, school, college and university rolled into one. They've got everything here!"

"But, surely you went to college yourself," said Astra. "COSMIC don't let you join their training course if you haven't been to college."

Dan blushed. "My mum and dad insisted I was taught at home – alone."

"I was Master Dan's teacher from his first day at school until his last," proclaimed Volt proudly. "And he received quite an impressive education, even if I do say so myself."

"I get it ..." grinned Astra. "You studied hard, but didn't get the chance to play hard."

Dan nodded. "Exactly."

"Oh, I don't know about that, Master Dan," said Volt. "Remember our monthly chess tournaments? They could be quite exciting, if I remember correctly."

Dan sighed. "I just want to go to one college party! Please?"

"Alright," said Astra. "But we're here to congratulate Honey on her graduation first."

"Of course," promised Dan.

"Then fasten your seatbelt, Dan Fireball!" said Astra, tapping the landing sequence into her keyboard. "You're going to a party!"

CHAPTER 2

EDUCATE!

Dan, Astra and Volt stepped out of the HS Infinity. All around them were tall, impressive buildings. Bright light shone from the clouds above.

"This is one of the oldest universities on the planet," Volt explained as they began to explore. "As Master Dan correctly said earlier, they teach all ages — from nursery to school leavers."

"Everyone's so small!" exclaimed Dan as a group of students hurried past. They were each around three years old, dressed in brightly coloured clothes.

"Those will be first years," said Astra. "And you were that small once, you know."

"Indeed he was, Miss Astra," said Volt. "In fact, I have some photographs here if you would care to see them."

"No!" cried Dan. "We ... er ... don't have time for that. We have to find Astra's cousin Honey and say hello."

Astra did her best to hide her smile. "She's studying astrophysics, so she'll probably be in the science department."

"Is that where the party is, afterwards?" asked Dan.

"I've no idea," said Astra. "And I don't want you going on about that all day. We're here to relax, remember?"

"You've told me often enough," grumbled Dan. "Hey!" he shouted as he was forced to jump out of the way as a baby in a colourful plastic walker dashed past.

"Sorry!" called the baby. "I'm late for my genetics class!"

"Genetics?" repeated Dan. "Things are really different in schools these days. I didn't start crossing different animals until I was nearly eight! Volt and I mixed a British bulldog with a particularly lazy sloth. We called the new animal a bull-dozer!"

"Education is always changing, Master Dan," said Volt. "It wasn't too many centuries ago that children started school aged five and left when they turned 18. Even later if they went on to college or university."

"They must have been really dim if it took them all those years," Dan commented.

"They didn't have speed learning in those days," said Astra.

"Really?" said Dan. "Then how did they find out about things?"

"They got their information from books," said Astra. "And they had teachers to help them — adult teachers."

Dan shuddered. "Then I'm very glad I'm a 23rd century boy."

"Astra!" cried a voice. "Astra!"

Astra looked up to see a girl of around seven years of age waving to her from a window high above. "Honey!" she shouted. "There you are!"

"Come up!" called Honey. "I'll meet you in my lab."

Honey Moon gave Astra, Dan and Volt a guided tour of the science department on their way to the graduation ceremony. They passed classrooms filled with young children — all wearing headphones and staring at flickering images rising up from hologram cubes.

"We use the latest speed learning equipment here on Neptune," Honey explained. "In fact, we've just upgraded the software to help the brightest students complete their courses a whole year earlier than before."

"That's all we need," whispered Dan to Volt. "Some super-smart nine-year-olds joining COSMIC and trying to get our jobs."

"What are these kids studying?" asked Astra, peering into a classroom which seemed to contain as many cats as children.

"They're a mixed ability group," Honey explained. "They'll be doing everything from 'C is for cat' to cloning the class kitten in one term. I was doing a little revision with my fellow graduates with them just before you arrived." She checked her watch. "Now, we'd better get to the school hall for the ceremony!"

Twenty minutes later Dan and Astra were among an audience of proud parents. Graduating students took to the stage one at a time to receive their diplomas from the principal of the university — a fair-haired 13-year-old boy.

Volt wheeled back and forth behind the seating, filming the ceremony on Astra's handheld computer.

Eventually, it was Honey's turn to climb up the steps and accept her degree. She shook hands with the principal, then approached the microphone. The audience slowly stopped clapping and fell silent.

"That's funny," said Dan. "I didn't think the students gave speeches."

"They don't," said Astra, shuffling nervously in her seat. "What's she doing?"

Everyone in the room watched as Honey grabbed hold of the microphone stand to steady herself. Then she cleared her throat and began to speak in a low, croaky voice. "Eeh! My feet are killing me!" she moaned. "Covered in bunions, they are. All down to these rotten winters we get on Neptune, I reckon."

"She's not wrong!" cried another of the young graduates from her seat. "The damp makes my bones ache!"

"Some days, I can't even make it to the shops and back for a loaf of bread and a packet of butterscotch sweets!" added another.

The audience listened in amazement to the comments made by the rest of Honey's classmates:

"It's not like it was back in my day!"

"Kids today – they don't know they're born!"

"We had it tough!"

"Is it time for my nap yet?"

The audience began to mutter unhappily to each other, wondering what was going on.

"They all sound like … adults!" hissed Dan to Astra. "Really old adults!"

Astra jumped up. "Honey!" she cried, racing for the stage. "What's going on?"

But before Honey could reply, a new figure appeared through the stage curtains. It was an adult, wearing comfy slippers and a grey cardigan.

Astra skidded to a halt. "The Geezer!" she exclaimed.

"The one and only!" The Geezer smiled. He snatched the microphone away from Honey. "Ladies and gentlemen ... I expect you're wondering what has happened to your darling children?"

A wave of "Yes" swept across the crowd.

"Allow me to explain." continued The Geezer. "You see, I've turned them all into old-aged pensioners!"

CHAPTER 3

HACK ATTACK

"**Y**our children are children no longer," announced The Geezer. "And they never will be again!"

"You monster!" cried a voice from the back of the hall. "Why have you done this?"

"To make sure there isn't a new generation of annoying kids to take control of the Solar System!" The Geezer replied. "When the current crop of children retires at the age of 18, there will be no one to take their place — just millions of old-before-their-time pensioners with nothing to do but moan about the weather! You'll be begging sensible adults like me to leave our retirement homes and run the place again."

"That's what you think!" cried Dan, running for the stage. "You're under arrest for … doing this!"

"Stop right there!" shouted The Geezer. "You can't arrest me today, Dan Fireball. COSMIC Captains cannot take prisoners on their day off — it's against the rules."

Dan turned to Astra. "Is that true?"

"Of course it's not true, you dummy!" roared Astra. "Get him!"

Dan made for the stage again, charging up the steps two at a time. But The Geezer's lie had given him enough time to disappear back behind the curtains. By the time Dan and Astra reached the backstage area, there was no sign of their target.

"Lost him again!" snapped Dan.

Astra hurried back to Honey, who she found sitting in a chair with a tartan blanket across her lap. "Are you okay?" she asked kindly.

"Okay?" said Honey. "Okay? Of course I'm not okay! I've just found out that there's no bingo on this week, and someone's helped themselves to the last biscuit in the biscuit tin! There are a couple of crispbreads left — but I can't eat them. Not with my teeth!"

Astra took Honey's hands and squeezed them. "Don't worry," she said. "We'll find out what The Geezer has done to you and your classmates, and we'll fix it."

But Honey was already fast asleep, snoring softly.

"I'm afraid it is not just Honey's class whose minds have been turned old." said Volt. "It appears that every student at Neptune Nursery is showing the same symptoms. They have all become old people."

"This is terrible!" said Dan. "I can't go partying with a bunch of old pensioners!" He caught Astra's stern gaze and added:

"Not when we have so many people to help!"

"How has The Geezer done this?" Astra demanded.

"He had that body clock gadget when we battled with him on Uranus," Dan pointed out. "Remember he used it to trick the dead into thinking they were still alive?"

"That can't be it," said Astra. "I've got that gadget now and, even if he'd made another one, moving the students' body clocks so far forward would age them physically as well as mentally. They'd look old as well, but they don't."

"I believe I may have the solution, Miss Astra," said Volt. "When we were touring the science department, I took the liberty of plugging myself into the university's speed learning computer in order to update myself on the latest advances in physics."

Astra nodded. "And …?"

"And it appears that the software used in the speed learning system has been hacked and replaced with a corrupted version."

"Of course!" cried Astra. "The Geezer is using the students' headphones to age their minds as they learn!"

"Hang on," said Dan. "Doesn't every department here use the same speed learning system?"

"They do," said Astra grimly. "Which means we're now standing on the planet of the pensioners!

"Sounds like a bad horror movie," said Dan.

"It will be if we can't reverse the process," said Astra.

"I have managed to download a fresh copy of the software," said Volt, producing a hologram cube.

"Brilliant!" cried Dan. "So, we can just replace the dodgy software with the correct version, pop everyone back on their headphones and reverse the process."

"I'm afraid it may not be that simple, Master Dan," said Volt. "You would have to upload the software from the computer The Geezer used to hack into the system, which I suspect will be located on his spaceship."

"We'd be spotted before we got anywhere near his ship," groaned Astra.

"Not if we were to go back to school first …" said Volt.

CHAPTER 4

YOUNG AGAIN

"We're going to do what?" Dan cried.

"Disguise ourselves as kids in order to get close enough to The Geezer's computer," said Astra. "It's our only chance to reset the software and give everyone on Neptune their childhood back."

"I get that bit!" said Dan. "But when you said 'disguise' — I thought you meant we'd be dressing up, maybe wearing a wig or a fake moustache."

"I fear that such a poor costume would never fool someone as clever as The Geezer," said Volt.

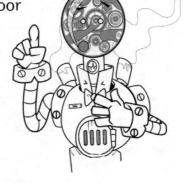

"So," said Astra, unclipping what looked like a TV remote control from her utility belt. "We're going to use this instead."

"How does it work?" asked Dan.

Volt took the gadget and pointed to a data display filled with numbers. "Everyone in the Solar System has a body clock," he explained. "Even robots such as myself. This body clock starts when we are born, controls how fast we will grow and regulates, eventually, when we will die."

"And this gizmo we nicked from The Geezer can alter that?"

"That is correct," said Volt. "Using this dial, we can slow down, speed up or even reverse our body clocks."

"And we're going to use it to turn ourselves back into toddlers again?" said Dan.

"I've already started the process, sir," said Volt.

"Really?" said Dan. "But, I don't feel any — Whoa! Is it just me, or is the room becoming bigger all of a sudden?"

"It's you!" said Astra. "You're shrinking. We all are."

"The feeling is most unusual!" said Volt as he grew smaller and smaller.

After a few seconds, two very young children and a small, fresh-off-the-assembly-line robot stood where the Space Hopper team had just been.

"That was funny!" exclaimed baby Astra in a squeaky voice.

Little puffs of steam rose up from Volt's tiny exhaust pipes. "I feel brand new again!" said the robot.

"I need a wee wee!" complained Dan.

"Here are some toddler clothes the principal gave me from the lost property box," said Astra. "Once we're dressed up, that bad Geezer man will think we're just kids who go to school here."

"Can I have another pair of trousers, please?" asked Dan.

"Why?" said Astra.

"I just did that wee wee!" moaned Dan.

Twenty minutes later, they approached the entrance to Shady Acres — The Geezer's stolen retirement home spaceship.

"Remember," whispered Astra. "We have to be old like grandmas and grandads."

"That's easy!" said Dan. "My grandad used to wee himself all the time!"

Volt picked the lock on the door, and they all crept inside. "This way ..."

The group tiptoed through the ship until they arrived at the command deck. Standing at one of the computer terminals was The Geezer himself.

"He looks a lot bigger now!" hissed Dan, nervously.

"There it is!" hissed Astra, pointing to a square-shaped hole on The Geezer's desk. "That's where Volt has to reset the speed learning software."

The robot held out the hologram cube which contained the clean version of the educational program. "I'll need a distraction to get in there," he whispered.

"No problem ..." said Astra. Then, she hurried straight over to The Geezer and pulled on his trouser leg. "Hey, you ..."

The Geezer looked down to find two toddlers standing at his feet. "What are you doing in here?" he demanded.

"We're looking for electric blankets and toffee you can chew without your teeth in!"said Dan in an old person's voice.

While The Geezer explained that any electric blankets they found on board Shady Acres were his property, Volt wheeled silently over to the square-shaped hole and slotted his cube into the slot. Then, with a click of the computer mouse, the speed learning software began to reset itself.

Astra pulled her communication bracelet out from under her sleeve. "We've done it!" she shouted into the microphone.
"Get everyone o put their headphones back on, now!"

"What?" cried The Geezer, spinning back to his computer display. He roared with anger when he saw all the students he had aged, changing back to their younger, inner selves. He tried to snatch up the hologram cube, but it was locked in place.

"You've ruined everything!" he roared.

"No," said Baby Dan, pulling the body clock gadget from the back of his nappy and twisting the dial. "We've fixed everything!"

Instantly, Dan, Astra and Volt grew back to their normal sizes.

"Space Hoppers!" The Geezer snarled.

"You look surprised." said Dan to The Geezer.

"And you look ridiculous!" smirked The Geezer.

Dan looked down and realised he was wearing toddler clothes and a nappy. "We forgot to bring our COSMIC uniforms with us," Dan groaned.

"Hopeless as ever!" snarled The Geezer, then he pushed Dan and Astra to the ground and ran out of the room.

"After him!" cried Astra, climbing back to her feet. They raced through Shady Acres and ran out of the back door into the bright Neptune daylight.

The Geezer was standing, rooted to the spot, as hundreds of angry students – now restored to children once more – marched towards him.

"We've got him now!" shouted Astra.

Dan stepped up to the evil adult. "Geezer!" he announced. "You are under arrest for messing with the heads of every student on Neptune – and for almost ruining my chances of going to a good party!"

He produced his handcuffs and tried to snap one end over The Geezer's wrist – but the handcuffs just went straight through.

"What's going on?" demanded Dan, reaching out towards his prisoner, but his hand also sank through The Geezer's body.

Then Dan's foot accidentally kicked against something on the ground.

"It's a hologram cube!" cried Astra, bending to pick it up. Instantly, the three-dimensional image of The Geezer flickered and disappeared.

Just then the door to Shady Acres retirement home slammed shut behind them, and the engines burst into life. "You'll never catch me, Dan Fireball!" cried The Geezer's voice through the ship's speakers. "Even if you live to be an old-aged pensioner!"

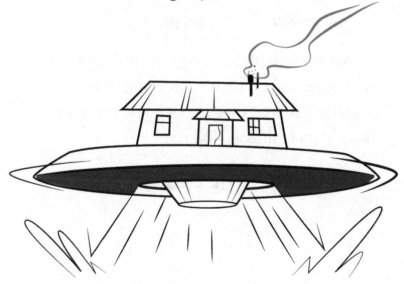

With a deafening roar, the retirement home took off and disappeared through the thin clouds above.

"We've lost him again!" exclaimed Dan. "Right – that's it! I'm going off to find a party right now!" He thrust the body clock gadget into Astra's hands and stormed away.

"Should I go after him, Miss Astra?" asked Volt.

"No," said Astra, grinning. "He'll be back any minute now."

Volt frowned. "How do you know?"

Astra watched Dan stride off, his nappy wobbling and his flesh bulging out of his toddler clothes. "They're not going to let him in anywhere dressed like that!"

THE END

Now read *Victory for Venus* to find out what The Geezer gets up to next!

GLOSSARY

assembly line — a way of making things in a factory by passing them along a line and adding parts one at a time

astrophysics — the study of how stars are made

bunion — a sore bit on the foot, often on the big toe

cloning — making an exact copy of a living thing

diploma — a certificate to show that a course of study has been completed

genetics — the study of how living things grow and develop

graduate — someone who has finished studying at a university

holographic — something made into a 3D picture using lasers

sequence — a list of instructions in a particular order

symptom — a sign of illness or something being wrong

QUIZ QUESTIONS

1   Why did the Space Hoppers go to Neptune in the first place?

2   Who was Dan's teacher?

3   What is the name of Astra's cousin?

4   How old was Dan when he started to do genetics in class?

5   How old is the principal of the university?

6   Who is responsible for turning all the graduates into old-aged pensioners?

7   How has he aged the minds of the graduates?

8   What disguise are the Space Hoppers going to use to get close enough to The Geezer's ship?

9   Why could Dan not put the handcuffs on The Geezer?

10 Why does Astra think that Dan will come back in a minute?

ABOUT THE AUTHOR

Tommy Donbavand writes full-time and lives in Lancashire with his family. He is also the author of the 13-book *Scream Street* series (currently in production for TV) and has written numerous books for children and young adults.

For Tommy, the best thing about being an author is getting to spend his days making up adventures for his readers. He also writes for 'The Bash Street Kids' in *The Beano*, which excites him beyond belief!

Find out more about Tommy and his other books at www.tommydonbavand.com

QUIZ ANSWERS

1 To spend their day off there.
2 Volt
3 Honey
4 Nearly eight
5 13
6 The Geezer
7 Hacked into the speed learning system and replaced it with a corrupted version.
8 Reverse their body clocks to become toddlers.
9 Because it was just a hologram of The Geezer.
10 Because he won't be able to get into a party dressed as a toddler.